D0578285

A Visit to the Big House

Oliver Butterworth

Illustrated by Susan Avishai

Houghton Mifflin Company

Boston 1993

Published in 1987 as *Una Visita a la Casa Grande/A Visit to the Big
House,* by Families in Crisis, Inc., and the Junior League of Hartford,
Connecticut. Thanks to both for their cooperation.

Library of Congress Cataloging-in-Publication Data

Butterworth, Oliver,
    A visit to the big house/Oliver Butterworth; illustrated by
Susan Avishai.
        p.   cm.
    Summary: Mother, Rose, and Willy go to prison to visit Daddy for
the first time.
    ISBN 0-395-52805-4
    [1. Prisons — Fiction.   2. Prisoners — Fiction.   3. Fathers —
Fiction.]   I. Avishai, Susan, ill.   II. Title
PZ7.B9823Vi   1993   92-9787
[E] — dc20   CIP
                           AC
Printed in the United States of America
HOR   10   9   8   7   6   5   4   3   2   1

A Visit to the Big House

Every Saturday, Mother made pancakes for breakfast. Rose was seven, and she always helped. Willy was five, and he got to make one pancake, but Mother held his hand so the pancake would land in the frying pan, not somewhere else.

Right in the middle of their Saturday breakfast, Mother said, "Do you know what we're going to do today?"

"No, what?" Rose and Willy asked.

"We're going to visit Daddy," Mother said.

"Can we?" Rose said.

Willy didn't say anything.

"Yes, we can," Mother said. "It's our first visiting day. From now on, we can visit every two weeks. We'll go there right after lunch, and we can spend an hour with him."

Willy still didn't say anything. He was looking down at his plate, and his mouth was shut tight.

"Come on, Willy," Mother said. "Let's finish up your breakfast."

"I don't want to go," said Willy.

Mother sighed. "But Willy, your daddy *wants* to see you and talk with you. It's been a whole month since he went up there, and he hasn't seen us in all that time."

Willy pouted. "I don't want to go see him in any old prison," he said.

"Willy," Rose said, "how would *you* feel if you were in prison, and your family didn't come to see you?"

"I'd feel sad," Willy said.

"Well, then," Rose said, "that's why we're going

to see him, so he won't be all sad and lonely."

Willy shook his head slowly. "But I don't want to see him in prison, 'cause that makes him look like a bad man, and I don't want to think he's a bad man."

Mother took his hands in hers. "I see what you mean, Willy," she said. She looked into his face. "Do you remember when you took that package of chewing gum from the drugstore?"

Willy nodded.

"And do you remember what Daddy and I did after we found out about it?"

Willy nodded again.

"What did we have you do?" Mother asked.

"We went back to the store," Willy said, "and I gave the chewing gum back to Mr. Angelo, and I told him I was sorry I stole the gum, and I wouldn't do it again."

"And what did Mr. Angelo say?"

Willy looked up at his mother. "He said I did the right thing to bring the gum back, and that maybe I'd learned something."

Willy's mother put her arms around him and slid him into her lap. "When you took the chewing gum, did that make you a bad person?"

"Nnnnnnnooooooooooooo," Willy said slowly.

"And was it a good thing to make up for what you had done?"

"Yes," Willy said.

Mother held him tight. "Well, Willy, your daddy took something that didn't belong to him, and going to prison is a way to make up for what he did."

She turned away so Willy wouldn't see her face.

"Don't cry, Mommy," Rose said.

"I'm trying not to," Mother said, "and I hope that Daddy learns something from this." She looked back at Willy and blinked her eyes a few times.

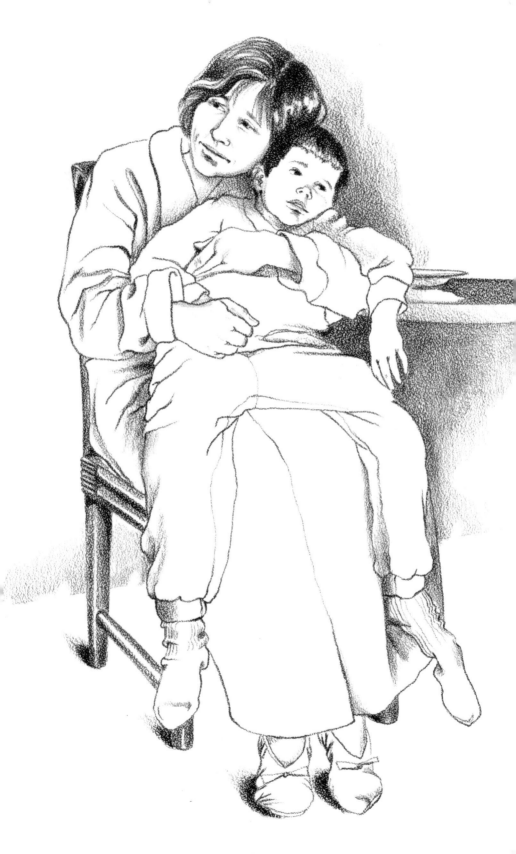

"All right," she said, "let's get the cleaning done, and then we'll have lunch, and then we'll go off to see Daddy." She looked at Rose and Willy. "It's a pretty long drive up there, so let's take along those drawing pads and the box of crayons. That will give you something to do in the car."

As they were driving to the prison, their old car made a clunky noise in the rear end.

"I don't know why it makes that noise," Mother said. "If Daddy was home, he'd know how to fix it. I suppose I'll have to take it to the garage, and that will cost a lot of money. Oh, dear!"

"How do we get to see Daddy?" Rose wanted to know. "Do they bring him out to talk to us?"

"No," Mother said. "They wouldn't do that. We'll talk to him in the prison visiting room."

"We go *into* the prison?" Rose said. "Are you sure they'll let us out again?"

"Of course," said Mother. "What would they want to keep us there for? We haven't done anything wrong."

"But we're his *family*," Rose said. "Maybe they'd blame us too."

Mother shook her head. "It doesn't work that way. The person who does something wrong goes to prison, not his family."

Willy was frowning. "Is he going to have chains on his arms and legs?"

"No, Willy," Mother said. "They don't wear chains nowadays."

"But I saw pictures of people in a dudgeon, and they all had chains on."

Mother smiled a little. "Not in a *dudgeon,* Willy. It's a *dungeon.* And that was in the old times. They don't have chains and dungeons now."

"What will he be wearing?" Rose wanted to know. "Those pajama things with big stripes?"

"No, Rose," Mother said. "Not stripes. Just a kind of uniform. I think it's brown — you know, a brown shirt and brown pants. But we'll see when we get there."

"What do they get to eat?" Willy said.

"We'll ask him that when we see him," Mother said. "He can tell us all about it."

They drove into the prison parking lot. Then they got out of the car and walked toward the gate. There was a high wire fence all around the prison, and a small brick house just behind the gate.

Rose was nervous. "Is that the prison?" she whispered.

"No," Mother said. "That's just the gatehouse. The prison is the big house behind it."

Inside the gatehouse, there was a guard in a blue uniform who asked them their names. Willy looked up at the guard with a serious face and said, "I'm going to visit my daddy."

"Good for you," said the guard, and he gave them a piece of paper to take with them. Mother signed her name in a book.

They walked through a gate in the high fence and along a sidewalk that led up to the big prison building. They went into a waiting room, where there were a lot of people sitting on benches. Several guards stood by a sliding door on the other side of the room. The door made a loud sound as it opened and shut.

Rose and Willy spent the time looking at the other families in the waiting room. The families sat on the benches, and the older children read comic books or stared at the floor. The small children wriggled around or stood up on the bench and watched the other children. Now and then someone would fall off a bench and cry for a while. The guard would call out a name every few minutes, and another family would go out through the sliding door.

ATTENTION

Parents are responsible for their childrens behavior in the visiting Center. No food, beverages or cigarettes are to leave the center

ATENCION

Finally Rose and Willy heard the guard call out their name, and Mother took them by the hand and walked toward the sliding door. Rose suddenly stopped and pulled at her mother's arm.

"I'm scared, Mommy," she said. "I don't want to go in there. It's dangerous!"

Mother smiled calmly at her and held tight to her hand. Willy leaned toward her and whispered loudly, "Don't be afraid, Rose! Just look 'em in the eye and they won't hurt you."

One of the guards at the door winked at Willy and slid the door open. When they had gone through, it rolled shut with a bang. They walked down a bare hall with a shiny floor, then into a long room with people sitting at tables, talking to men in brown uniforms on the other side of the tables.

Mother and Rose and Willy sat down at an empty table, and their daddy came and sat down in front of them. He didn't look happy, but he smiled and said hello.

"Hey, everybody, I'm so glad to see you all again. How are you, anyway? You're looking good, Willy, but Rose, you look kind of nervous. And Mommy, how's it going with you? You have a lot of work on your hands, I bet."

Rose and Willy looked at Daddy, and Mother said, "The children have been a lot of help, and things are going all right, but the car is making a funny sound. Should I take it to the garage?"

"I guess you better," Daddy said.

Rose thought he looked worried but was trying to be cheerful. Willy stared at him across the table.

"Well," Daddy said, "how's school going, Rose? Do you like your teacher?"

"Yes," Rose said. "She told us to write about what we did to help at suppertime, and I wrote what Mommy did and what I did and what Willy did, and I said that our daddy was away."

Her daddy didn't look happy at that. "Did you say where I was?"

"No," Rose said. "I just said you were away."

"I see," Daddy said, and looked at Mother.

Willy leaned forward on the table. "What do they give you to eat, Daddy?"

"Oh," Daddy said, "the food's OK, Willy. It's regular stuff, like eggs or cereal for breakfast, and spaghetti or ham or chicken for other meals, and guess what we have for dessert sometimes?"

"Bread and water?" Willy asked.

Daddy grinned. "Come on, Willy, they don't do that now. You must have been watching some TV show. What they give us sometimes is pie with ice cream. That's my favorite."

"Wow," Willy said. "That's pretty cool."

"Yeah," Daddy said, but he had stopped smiling. "It isn't all that great, Willy. I'd much rather be at home with you folks. I really miss you guys, you know? And I've got to be here for two years, even with good behavior."

Daddy didn't look happy, so Rose asked him if the people in prison had to do any work.

"Oh, yes," Daddy said. "There's all kinds of work. My job is in the print shop. We do signs and printing for the state, and we even get out a little newspaper for the prison here. I wrote an article for it last week. Everybody here has a job of some sort. It just wouldn't be healthy if everyone just sat around waiting for their time to be up. The people here do the cooking, auto repair, laundry, cleaning, just about everything."

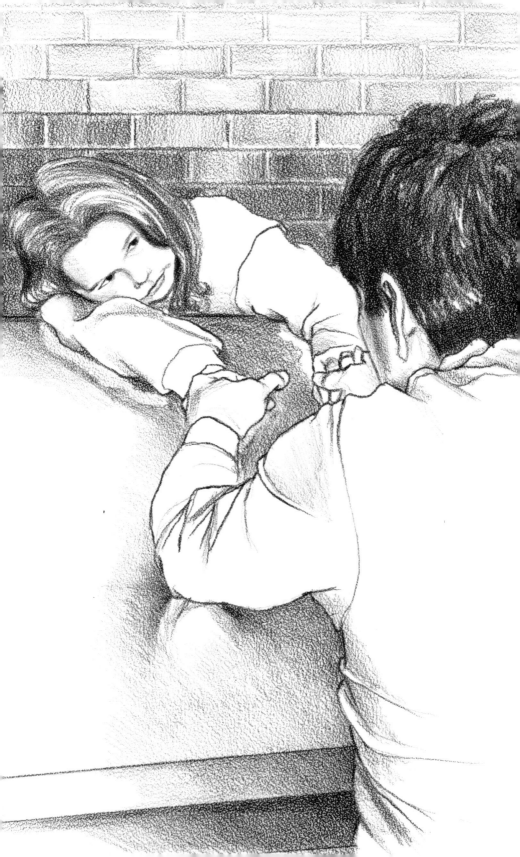

Daddy took a lot of time telling them about all the jobs there were to do at the prison — and the volunteer jobs like tutoring people in reading — and about playing volleyball and jogging.

Then a guard came over and tapped Daddy on the shoulder.

"Time's up," the guard said.

Daddy got up and hugged Rose and Willy and Mother. "So long, kids," he said. "See you all in two weeks, OK?"

On the way home, Rose and Willy drew pictures with the crayons they had brought along. It was pretty quiet in the car for a while, and then Mother asked them about their pictures.

Willy said he had drawn a picture of Daddy sitting at the table. "He looks a little sad because he's not at home with us. But not *too* sad, because he's doing the right thing, and he's learned something. And, Mommy, can I take my picture to kindergarten to show my teacher?"

His mother looked at him and didn't say anything for a minute. Then she said, "All right, Willy. I think that would be a good thing to do."

Rose said, "I drew a picture of the big house Daddy is living in, and he's looking out the window and waving to us. He's a little sad because he has to live in the big house, but he's smiling because he knows we're coming to visit him again."

Mother smiled at both of them. "You're nice children," she said. "It won't be easy for these two years, but we'll all work hard, and we'll manage until Daddy comes back to us again."

And the car didn't make any clunky sounds all the way home.